AIDEN'S
DINOSAUR ADVENTURES

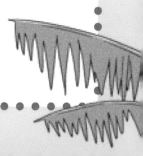

Library of Congress Control Number: 2020920394

HARDBACK: 9781953791245
PAPERBACK: 9781953791238
EBOOK: 9781953791252

Ordering Information:

For orders and inquiries, please contact:
1-888-404-1388
www.goldtouchpress.com
book.orders@goldtouchpress.com

Printed in the United States of America

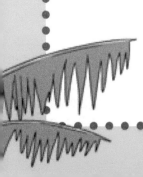

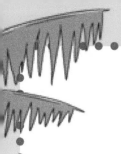

AIDEN'S
DINOSAUR ADVENTURES

DIANE MILES GRIFFIN

ILLUSTRATED BY

GABRIEL PARAME

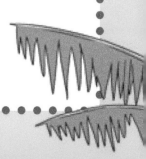

It was Saturday morning, and Aiden was up, ready to go the museum. His teacher sent a note home on Friday about a dinosaur exhibit on Saturday at the local museum. The principal gave the teachers free tickets to give to each child in the class.

Wearing his dinosaur pajamas, Aiden ran down the hall from his bedroom into the kitchen. "Mommy, Mommy, today is Saturday," he yelled. "I want to see the dinosaurs. Can you take me to see them?"

Mom was in the kitchen making breakfast. She made pancakes in the shape of a T. rex. It was Aiden's favorite dinosaur. She also cut apple slices in the shape of a stegosaurus. "I want to see the big T. rex, the stegosaurus, the triceratops, and—"

"Okay, okay," said Mom, "but first, you must eat your breakfast, take a bath, and get dressed."

Aiden ate his dinosaur pancakes. He played with his apple slices before he ate them and drank his orange juice, which he called Dino juice.

"Mom, can you buy some dinosaur eggs for me from the store at the museum?"

"We'll see," said Mom. "Now finish your breakfast so you can take a bath and get dressed."

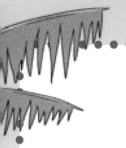

Aiden enjoyed bath time. Mom put blue "dino" soap in his bath water. He loaded the tub with dinosaurs of all kinds. "Mom," he shouted from the bathroom, "can you bring my stegosaurus and T. rex?"

"You have enough dinosaurs in the tub already," Mom shouted back.

"But I want my stegosaurus and T. rex," Aiden cried.

"You will have to take some of the other dinosaurs out," she said.

Mom brought the two dinosaurs into the bathroom. "Two will have to come out," she said.

"But I want them to stay," said Aiden.

"Two will have to come out, or you can't have these," said Mom.

"All right," he said slowly. He took out two of the dinosaurs and handed them to Mom. She gave him the stegosaurus and the T. rex.

"Ten more minutes," she said, "and you'll have to get out of the tub and get dressed."

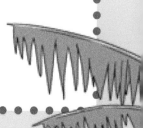

Mom helped Aiden with his clothes. He put on dinosaur underwear, khaki shorts, and a white T-shirt with a big T. rex on the front of it. His socks had little dinosaurs on them, and he had a small dinosaur on each shoe. "Mom, will Dad be there?"

"Yes," she said, "he'll meet us there, then he will have to go back to work."

Aiden's bedroom was decorated with dinosaur curtains on the window. On his bed were dinosaur sheets and a pillow with a picture of a T. rex on it.

He had dinosaurs on the wall, big ones and small ones. He even had a dinosaur rug on the floor, not to mention stuffed dinosaurs and action figures all over the room. Mom looked at Aiden when he had finished getting dressed. "Dinosaur palooza, you're going to turn into a dinosaur," she said.

"Roar-r-r-r," he shouted. "Then I can scare my friends when they come to visit."

Mom shook her head and let out a big sigh. "Time to go, my little Aidenosaurus," she said.

"Roar-r-r-r," went Aiden all the way to the car.

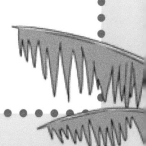

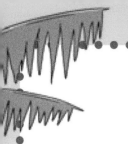

Aiden played with his T. rex as he rode in the back seat of the car. After a while, he put it down. "Are we there yet?" he asked.

"We'll be there in a few minutes," said Mom. When she drove into the parking lot, Aiden looked out the window. He saw a long line of children and their parents waiting to go inside the museum. Mom parked the car. Then she went to get Aiden out of his car seat, but before she could get him out, he had already unbuckled himself.

"Come on, Mommy," he said. "We have to go in now!" Mom took Aiden by the hand, and they walked to the end of the line. "Let's go in," said Aiden.

"We can't go in now—we have to wait in line just like the other children and their parents."

"Why?" asked Aiden.

"It's not fair to get in front of other people when they are in line," Mom said.

"I want to see the dinosaurs now!" said Aiden.

"We have to wait in line until it's our time to go in," said Mom. Aiden was not happy about waiting in line. He folded his arms and began to pout.

Suddenly, a big T. rex walked by, greeting the children. Some were happy to see it, while others were scared and clung to their parents. When Aiden saw the dinosaur, he began to cry. "I don't want to see the dinosaurs," he cried.

"It will be all right," Mom told him. "That's just someone in a dinosaur costume."

When they got closer to the door to go in, Aiden heard loud sounds coming from inside the museum. "I don't want to go in," he cried.

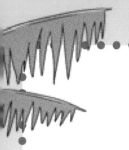

Inside the museum were lots of tall trees and plants with big, wide leaves. Dinosaurs big and small were everywhere. In the middle of the museum was a tall T. rex making loud roaring sounds that filled the room. Smoke was coming out of a volcano on the far side of the museum. Aiden clung closer to his dad when he heard the roar of the T. rex. Mom walked beside them with her camcorder videoing everything as they made their way through the museum.

"Look," said Mom, "some children are walking around enjoying themselves. Don't you want to walk around like them?"

"No," said Aiden.

"It's okay," said Dad. "I'll hold your hand."

Aiden stayed close to his dad. Every time he heard a loud sound, he clung tightly to his dad's leg. After a few minutes, he began to feel better. He told his dad that he wanted to walk around like the other children, but he would have to stay close by. Dad and Mom agreed to walk with him.

As they walked through the museum, a man asked Aiden if he wanted to dig for dinosaur bones. "I think that is a great idea," said Dad.

"So do I," said Mom.

The man led Aiden to the station where other children were digging in sand for dinosaur bones. He gave Aiden some small tools and showed him how to dig in the sand. Soon, Aiden uncovered a plastic skeleton. The man told him that it was the bones of a T. rex. Aiden smiled and told him that T. rex was his favorite dinosaur. The man placed the skeleton in a box and put it in a bag with a big T. rex on it.

He gave the bag to Aiden. "Roar-r-r-r," said Aiden. He was very excited and wanted to see more things in the museum.

"Look, there's a dinosaur game station over there," Mom said. "Do you want to go there?"

"Yes!" shouted Aiden as he ran toward the games.

When they got to the game station, Aiden chose a game where he had to hit a dinosaur as it popped up from a hole. Each time he hit one, he won free tickets. They played another game where he also won tickets. He traded them in for a T. rex hat.

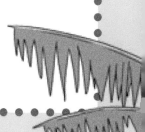

The family walked on, looking at different dinosaurs in their habitats. Aiden named every dinosaur he saw. They walked past a stegosaurus eating leaves from the bottom branch of a tree. Dad stopped to take a picture of Aiden as he stood by the stegosaurus. In the air, a pterodactyl was flying high above the trees.

When they reached the middle of the museum, there stood T. rex, roaring very loud. Aiden was afraid and wanted to leave. "We're right here," said Dad. "Why don't we take a picture beside the T. rex?"

"I'll take the picture for you," said a lady as she was passing by. "Say cheeseee."

Mom and Dad made a big smile. Aiden tried to smile, but he was still afraid. "One more," said the lady. "Smile." He finally gave a smile as the lady snapped the picture again.

They went to another station where Aiden made a dinosaur necklace. He put it on after he finished it. After leaving that station, he went to the painting station where he painted a picture of a T. rex. While they waited for the picture to dry, they decided to go to the store in the museum.

Mom bought the dinosaur eggs Aiden wanted. Dad bought a T-shirt with other dinosaurs on it and a T. rex in the middle. After that, they went back to the painting station.

The lady at the station put the picture in a frame that had dinosaur tracks around it and wrapped it in tissue paper. Mom took the picture and placed it in the bag along with the dinosaur bones, the hat, the dinosaur eggs,

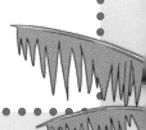

Outside the museum was a playground where the children could go to play. There was a big dinosaur bounce house where children could bounce and jump around. There was a dinosaur slide where they had to climb the stairs and slide down a big slide. There was also a dinosaur train that took the children all around the playground. It made loud dinosaur sounds as it went around the track.

Aiden was very excited. He ran to the bounce house. He got in line and waited his turn. Mom and Dad waited for him to get out. When he got out, he ran to the giant dinosaur slide. After that, he rode on the train with Mom and Dad. Then it was time to go.

Dad walked Aiden to the car and buckled him in his car seat. "See you later, little dino," he said. He kissed Aiden on the head and closed the door.

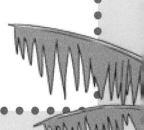

When Mom got in the car, Aiden was in the back seat looking at all the things he had in his bag. Mom gave him the juice from his bag. "Roar-r-r," he said, and he drank his juice. When he finished, he put the box in the cupholder. Then he checked to see if he still had on his dinosaur hat. He talked about all the things he saw and did that day. Mom smiled and listened while he talked.

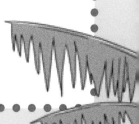

When they got home, Aiden was fast asleep. He had talked and played himself to sleep. Mom unbuckled him from the car seat and carefully took him out. She carried him and his bag into the house. She took him to his room and laid him on his bed. He was still wearing his dinosaur hat. Then Mom put a blanket over him. "What a day this has been," she said to herself. She kissed Aiden softly on the forehead. "Sleep well, my little Aidenosaurus."

Lightning Source UK Ltd.
Milton Keynes UK
UKHW052123271020
372323UK00002B/43